YOUR LAND
AND
MY LAND
ASIA

We Visit

INDIA

Khadija

Ejaz

Mitchell Lane
PUBLISHERS
P.O. Box 196
Hockessin, Delaware 19707

YOUR LAND AND MY LAND ASIA

Cambodia
China
India
Indonesia
Japan
Malaysia
North Korea
The Philippines
Singapore
South Korea

We Visit

INDIA

Mitchell Lane

PUBLISHERS

Printing   1   2   3   4   5   6   7   8   9

Asia

Library of Congress Cataloging-in-Publication Data
Ejaz, Khadija.
  We visit India / by Khadija Ejaz.
     pages cm. — (Your land and my land: Asia)
  Includes bibliographical references and index.
  ISBN 978-1-61228-477-4 (library bound)
  1. India—Juvenile literature. I. Title.
  DS407.E393 2013
  954—dc23
                                                    2013033971
eBook ISBN: 9781612285320

DEDICATION: To my Muslim grandparents who, for better or for worse, did not migrate to Pakistan in 1947.

PUBLISHER'S NOTE: This story is based on the author's extensive research, which she believes to be accurate. Documentation of this research is on page 61.

The internet sites referenced herein were active as of the publication date. Due to the fleeting nature of some websites, we cannot guarantee they will all be active when you are reading this book.

PBP

Contents

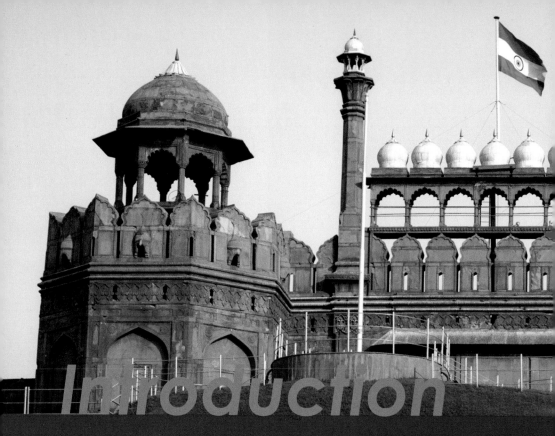

Introduction

Everything in India comes in multiples. The average Indian knows at least two languages, and some religious places draw followers from different religions. Many Indians even worship more than one deity. Indian life is far from monochromatic.

India has much in common with its mother continent with regard to its diversity. The country is located in Asia, which is the largest continent in the world. Asia forms one-third of the planet's land mass and is home to 60 percent of its people. Thousands of languages are spoken across Asia.

In the past, the Europeans used to refer to Asian societies as Oriental or Eastern and would loosely categorize them as Near Eastern, Middle Eastern, or Far Eastern (depending on their distance from Europe). Today, Asia is subdivided into North Asia, West Asia, Central Asia, South Asia, East Asia, or Southeast Asia.

India occupies a prominent place in South Asia. It is not the only country in South Asia, but its presence is so important that the region is also known as the Indian subcontinent. Let's learn more about this giant from South Asia.

The Red Fort in Delhi is part of an old walled city that was once the capital of the Mughal Empire.

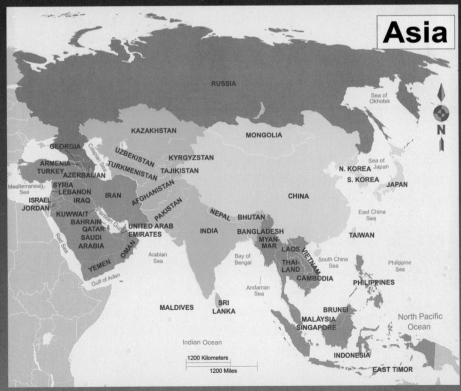

Asia

RUSSIA

KAZAKHSTAN

MONGOLIA

Sea of Okhotsk

N

GEORGIA

Caspian Sea

UZBEKISTAN

KYRGYZSTAN

ARMENIA
TURKEY
AZERBAIJAN

TURKMENISTAN

TAJIKISTAN

N. KOREA

Sea of Japan

S. KOREA

JAPAN

Mediterranean Sea

SYRIA
LEBANON
IRAQ

IRAN

AFGHANISTAN

CHINA

ISRAEL
JORDAN

Persian Gulf

PAKISTAN

NEPAL

BHUTAN

East China Sea

KUWAIT
BAHRAIN
QATAR
SAUDI
ARABIA

UNITED ARAB
EMIRATES

INDIA

BANGLADESH

MYAN-
MAR

TAIWAN

Red Sea

OMAN

Arabian Sea

Bay of Bengal

LAOS
THAI-
LAND

VIETNAM

South China Sea

Philippine Sea

YEMEN

Gulf of Aden

CAMBODIA

PHILIPPINES

Andaman Sea

MALDIVES

SRI
LANKA

BRUNEI

North Pacific Ocean

Indian Ocean

MALAYSIA
SINGAPORE

1200 Kilometers

1200 Miles

INDONESIA

EAST TIMOR

The Gateway of India overlooks the Arabian Sea in Mumbai. The arch was built to commemorate the arrival of Great Britain's King George V and Queen Mary in India in 1911.

Overview of India

Welcome to India! Many people are surprised to learn that the modern nation of India is not even 70 years old. Until gaining its independence on August 15, 1947, India had been dominated by the British for 200 years.

Jawaharlal Nehru, India's first Prime Minister, made a famous speech when the clock struck midnight and brought India its independence:

> At the stroke of the midnight hour, when the world sleeps, India will awake to life and freedom. A moment comes, which comes but rarely in history, when we step out from the old to the new, when an age ends, and when the soul of a nation, long suppressed, finds utterance. It is fitting that at this solemn moment we take the pledge of dedication to the service of India and her people and to the still larger cause of humanity.[1]

The people of India had been fighting for independence from the British for years. Young men and women—sometimes entire families—from different religious and economic backgrounds had fought together for the cause. Many had even lost their lives in its pursuit. After so many years, their sacrifices would not have been in vain.

But at the last moment, political events soured the celebrations. British India was split into two different countries, India and Pakistan, based primarily on the dominant religion in each country. The population of India was mostly Hindu, while Pakistan was predominantly

Jawaharlal Nehru, India's first prime minister, delivers his famous "tryst with destiny" speech towards midnight on August 14, 1947, at the Parliament House in New Delhi.

Muslim. The division was awkward. Pakistan was made up of East Pakistan and West Pakistan, with India stretching for more than 1,000 miles (1,600 kilometers) between the two regions. East Pakistan declared independence from West Pakistan in 1971 and became Bangladesh, while West Pakistan simply became Pakistan.

The Partition of 1947 caused considerable unrest in newly independent India and Pakistan, particularly in the form of violence between the two religions. Some people from the minority groups did not migrate and decided to risk staying in their new country. Many Hindus and Muslims chose to uproot themselves and leave everything behind because they didn't want to stay in a country where they would be the religious minority. Refugees flooded India and Pakistan from across their shared borders. This chaotic mass migration is the largest in world history and possibly the bloodiest. Over a million people lost their lives in attacks between the two religions.[2] The emotions of the migration can still be felt in India today, particularly in north India.

FYI FACT:

Unlike states, union territories are governed directly by the federal government in New Delhi. Their administrative officials are appointed by the president of India.

FYI FACT:

Many movies have been made about India and its people for American and British audiences. The best-known include *Gandhi* (1982), *City of Joy* (1992), *Bend It Like Beckham* (2002), *Bride and Prejudice* (2004), and *Life of Pi* (2012).

Today, India shares its borders with Pakistan in the west, China and Nepal in the north, and Burma, Bhutan, and Bangladesh in the east. The island nation of Sri Lanka is less than 20 miles (32 km) away from the southeast tip of India at its closest point. India is a peninsular nation, with water surrounding its triangular southern portion. Its western and eastern coastlines run along the Arabian Sea and the Bay of Bengal respectively. Its southernmost tip extends out into the Indian Ocean. The archipelagoes—large groups of islands—of Lakshadweep and Andaman and Nicobar also belong to India.

India's territory consists of 28 states and seven union territories. These regions are further divided into *zillas*. *Zillas* are made up of *tehsils*, which represent governance at the village level. India's capital is New Delhi, one of the most densely populated cities in the world. Some other major Indian cities are Mumbai (formerly Bombay), Kolkata (formerly Calcutta), Bengaluru (formerly Bangalore), and Chennai (formerly Madras).

Mumbai's famous Taj Mahal Palace Hotel opened in 1903. It is located across the street from the Gateway of India.

Where in the World

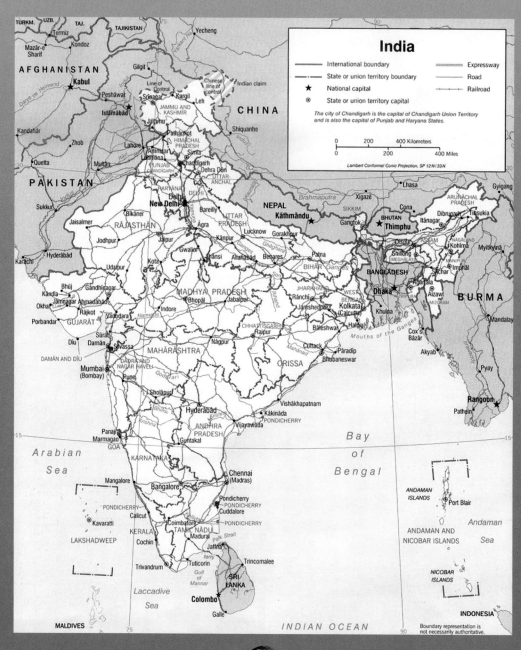

INDIA FACTS AT A GLANCE

Official Country Name: Republic of India

Official Language: Hindi, Bengali, Telugu, Marathi, Tamil, Urdu, Gujarati, Malayalam, Kannada, Oriya, Punjabi, Assamese, Kashmiri, Sindhi, and Sanskrit

Population: 1,205,073,612 (July 2012 estimate)

Land Area: 1,847,456 square miles (4,784,889 square kilometers); roughly one-third the size of the United States

Capital: New Delhi

Government: federal republic

Ethnic Makeup: Indo-Aryan 72%, Dravidian 25%, Mongoloid and other 3%

Religions: Hindu 80.5%, Muslim 13.4%, Christian 2.3%, Sikh 1.9%, other 1.8%, unspecified 0.1%

Exports: petroleum products, precious stones, machinery, iron and steel, chemicals, vehicles, apparel

Imports: crude oil, precious stones, machinery, fertilizer, iron and steel, chemicals

Crops: rice, wheat, oilseed, cotton, jute, tea, sugarcane, lentils, onions, potatoes

Average Temperatures: August 94.1°F (34.5°C), January 68.7°F (20.4°C)—Chennai on the southeastern coast; August 77°F (25°C); January 7°F (-14°C)—Leh in the mountains in the northern part of the country

Average Annual Rainfall: 463.7 inches (1,177.7 cm)—Cherrapunji in northeastern India, one of the wettest places on Earth; 8.35 inches (21.2 cm)—Jaisalmer in the Great Indian Desert near the border with Pakistan

Highest Point: Kanchenjunga—28,209 feet (8,598 meters)

Longest River: Ganga (or Ganges)—1,569 miles (2,525 kilometers)

National Flag: Three equal horizontal bands of saffron (top), white, and green, with a blue chakra (24-spoked wheel) centered in the white band. Saffron represents courage, sacrifice, and the spirit of renunciation. White signifies purity and truth. Green stands for faith and fertility. The blue chakra symbolizes the wheel of life in movement and death in stagnation

National Sport: None, but cricket is the most popular

National Flower: Lotus

National Bird: Indian peafowl

National Tree: Banyan

Source: CIA World Factbook: India
https://www.cia.gov/library/publications/the-world-factbook/geos/in.html

The Qutub Minar in Delhi gets its name from Qutub-ud-din Aibak, who ruled on behalf of Muhammad Ghori. Aibak would go on to become the first sultan of Delhi.

Ancient Invasions

Local tourism pamphlets call the iron pillar at the Qutub Complex in Delhi the "rustless wonder of India" because it does not corrode. That is truly a wonder because the pillar is almost 2,000 years old.[1] It weighs seven tons (6,350 kg) and is more than 23 feet (7 meters) high. Evidence suggests that it was brought from central India as a trophy.

The Qutub Complex houses many such monuments, the most recognizable of which is the Qutub Minar, a 239-feet-high (73 meters) minaret built in 1192. The Qutub Minar is the tallest brick minaret in the world and is listed by UNESCO as a World Heritage Site. It had been built to mark the victory of the Muslim Afghani invader Muhammad Ghori over the Hindu Rajput king Prithviraj Chauhan.

India's history is the story of the rise and fall of many kingdoms once scattered in and around South Asia. India also drew the attention of people from outside the region. Thousands of years of human interaction—migrations, invasions, wars, commerce, evangelism, and more—in South Asia are responsible for the layer upon diverse layer of culture that characterize India today. Before 1947, the word "India" loosely referred to a part of South Asia. British Prime Minister Winston Churchill said in a speech in 1931, "India is a geographical term. It is no more a united nation than the Equator."[2]

India's oldest civilization flourished around the Indus River in the northwestern part of the country around 2500-1500 BCE. The people of the Indus Valley built their towns in sophisticated grid layouts with elaborate drainage systems and were known to trade with ancient Egypt and Mesopotamia. Their most important cities were Harappa and Mohenjo-daro, whose remains are now in Pakistan. Other ruins are open to visitors at Lothal and Dholavira in the western Indian state of Gujarat. While the writing of the people of the Indus Valley has yet to be deciphered, many aspects of their life have trickled down the centuries to become part of modern Indian culture and religion.[3]

The religions of Hinduism, Buddhism, and Jainism trace their origins to India's Vedic Period, which flourished in the northern Indian plains from 2000 BCE until 500 BCE. The Hindu scriptures of the Vedas were written at this time. The plains were divided into 16 kingdoms, clumped together into four large states. According to a controversial theory, the Vedic people of north India were descended from Central Asian nomads called the Aryans, whose customs formed the basis of the modern Hindu religion. The theory also suggests that these nomads had lighter-colored skin than the Dravidian natives of India, whom they enslaved and caused to move to south India.[4]

South Asia was no stranger to invasions. The Persian king Darius had conquered the areas of Punjab and Sindh around the India-Pakistan border

Alexander the Great led his Greek army into India. The Greeks thought India marked the edge of the world.

in the 5th century BCE, and in 326 BCE, Alexander the Great extended his empire to the Beas River in north India.

India's first great empire was established in 322 BCE by the Mauryan king Chandragupta. At its greatest extent, the Mauryan Empire covered almost all of modern India and traded with ancient Rome and China. The capital of the empire was at Patliputra; its ruins can still be visited in the eastern Indian city of Patna, Bihar, today.

The most famous Mauryan ruler was Ashoka. Most Indians know him as Ashoka the Great, but in the early years of his reign, he was known for his cruelty. His fearsome torture chamber was called Ashoka's Hell, and Buddhist scriptures from that era remember him as Ashoka the Cruel. It was not until the bloody battle of Kalinga on India's eastern coast around 260 BCE that Ashoka had a crisis of conscience. The staggering loss of life he witnessed made him change his ways, and he gradually left Hinduism for Buddhism. For the rest of his reign, most of his efforts were directed at maintaining peace.

Powerful kingdoms in the south kept the Mauryan Empire at bay. Even then, the south maintained an identity distinct from the north.[5] The tribal territories along India's southern coastal plains were governed by local dynasties, such as the Cholas, Pandyas, Chalukyas, Cheras, and Pallavas. Their architecture was distinctive, and they maintained their own trading links with the Egyptians and the Romans.

India's Golden Age began with the establishment of the Gupta dynasty in 319 BCE. The rulers encouraged the pursuit of the arts and sciences, and India made great advances in fields like astronomy,

The iron pillar in Delhi. According to a local legend, people could earn good luck by standing with their back to the pillar and touching both arms after wrapping them around the pillar.

literature, architecture, mathematics, and technology. The iron pillar in Delhi is thought to have been constructed during this time.[6]

The Sanskrit poet Kalidasa and astronomer/mathematician Aryabhata lived during the Gupta Period. When India put its first satellite into space in 1975, it was named after Aryabhata, who, amongst his other works, discovered the zero and worked on the value of the mathematical constant pi (which is used to calculate the area and circumference of circles).

Repeated invasions by the Huns eroded the Gupta dynasty by the 6th century. India's Golden Age left a number of smaller Hindu kingdoms that fought each other for control in its wake, leaving the region vulnerable to foreign invaders. Mahmud of Ghazni from Afghanistan alone conducted 17 raids between 1001 and 1025. Another Afghan—Muhammad Ghori—conquered Delhi late in the 12th century. This laid the foundations of the Delhi Sultanate, which established Muslim control over a large part of India.

FYI FACT:

The national emblem of India was taken from the lion capital of the Ashoka pillar in Sarnath. The wheel—the Buddhist *dharmachakra*, the Wheel of Life—in the Indian national flag is also taken from the Ashoka pillar.

Humayun's tomb in Delhi. This 16th century Mughal structure became a UNESCO World Heritage Site in 1993. It is located near the mausoleum of the famous Sufi saint, Nizamuddin Auliya.

Muslims, Europeans, and Nationhood

The noises of the modern world cannot follow you to Hampi. Once the capital of the great Hindu kingdom of Vijayanagar, the ruins of Hampi today silently sit among rocky cliffs and dusty boulders along the Tungabhadra River in the southern state of Karnataka. Far away from Bengaluru, the cyber-capital of modern India, visitors can easily spend a few quiet days wandering about this eight-square-mile (21 sq. km) UNESCO World Heritage Site. Once upon a time, Hampi was home to over half a million people and reportedly boasted a million-man army. Pilgrims and travelers from as far away as Portugal and Persia filled the column-lined Bazaar Street, where holy deities are still carried in public for the Chariot Festival. The musical pillars of the Vitthala Temple still carry their tune. At the Virupaksha Temple, an elephant called Lakshmi will bless you with her trunk if you give her a coin.[1]

The Hindu Vijayanagar Empire rose to power in central India as the Delhi Sultanate in the north went into decline. In its last days, the sultanate suffered a terrible blow in 1398 when Delhi was raided by a Central Asian invader called Timur. The Vijayanagar Empire lasted well into the 16th century and became the most dominant Hindu power the south had ever seen.[2] Its decline was followed by the rise of the Muslim Mughal Empire, which at its peak, covered almost the whole of South Asia.

Babar of Kabul (in modern-day Afghanistan) founded the Mughal Empire in 1526 when he defeated the sultan of Delhi at the Battle of

Mughal emperor Shah Jahan was famous for his Peacock Throne. It was made of gold and studded with hundreds of rubies, emeralds, diamonds, and pearls. Today, the Koh-i-Noor diamond that was once part of the throne is set in the crown of Queen Elizabeth II and can be seen in the Tower of London.

Panipat. Babar's son Humayun was forced to retreat to Iran by Sher Shah Suri, a powerful Muslim ruler from eastern India, but returned to Delhi in 1555 after Suri's death. Humayun's tomb is a popular tourist spot in Delhi today.[3] The Taj Mahal in Agra and the Red Forts in both Agra and Delhi are other legacies from the Mughal era.

The Mughals extended their power in the south, but they faced opposition from the Hindu Marathas of central India and the Hindu Rajputs of western India. One of the most famous Maratha warriors was Shivaji, who founded the Maratha Empire in 1674. In 1996, the Victoria Terminus in Mumbai (also a UNESCO World Heritage Site) was renamed the Chhatrapati Shivaji Terminus. The city's international airport is also named after this Maratha hero.

By the 18th century, the Mughal Empire had weakened. The Christian Europeans had arrived in South Asia by then. The Portuguese explorer Vasco da Gama had discovered the sea route to India in 1498, and the Portuguese captured Goa soon after. In 1631, the British East India Company established its first trading post in India, and the French followed in 1672. The Swedes, the Danes, the Belgians, and the Dutch also traded with India.

British monarchs granted The East India Company exclusive British business rights in India. Despite swearing allegiance to the Mughals, the company grew powerful, particularly after opening its trading post in Kolkata in 1690.[4] In 1756, a local Muslim ruler attacked a British settlement in Kolkata and imprisoned his captives in a cramped dungeon. Many prisoners died overnight, which earned the dungeon the name of "the Black Hole of Kolkata." A year later, the ruler was overthrown by the military forces of the East India Company at the Battle of Plassey.

A hundred years later, Hindu and Muslim soldiers rebelled against their British superiors in north and central India after refusing to bite off rifle cartridges that were rumored to be greased with cow and pork fat. This sparked a number of rebellions across British India.

The Mutiny of 1857 did not defeat the British, however, and led to Queen Victoria officially extending her rule over India. She dissolved the East India Company and sent the last Mughal emperor, Bahadur

One of the most heroic figures from the Mutiny of 1857 was Rani Lakshmibai. She was the queen of Jhansi, a city in the north Indian state of Uttar Pradesh. Rani Lakshmibai was born in Varanasi, Uttar Pradesh, into a Marathi family and had married into the Jhansi royal family. By the time of the mutiny, she was already a young widow with a young son. She was only 30 when she died in 1858, but the people of India still remember her as the brave warrior queen who fought the British. Her palace in Jhansi, the Rani Mahal, is now a museum in her honor.

Shah II, into exile. The British Raj had arrived. This is the term for British rule in the Indian subcontinent for nearly 100 years, until India became independent. "Raj" means "royalty" or "kingdom" in Hindi and Sanskrit.

Indian resistance continued into the next century and reached its peak during World War II. The best-known face of the Indian independence movement was Mohandas Gandhi. He was born in Porbandar, Gujarat, in 1869 and went to law school in London. He practiced law in South Africa, but his experiences there with discrimination by white people against non-whites inspired him to return to India. Gandhi organized a number of protests against the British, and he encouraged all Indians to boycott foreign-made goods and dress in Indian *khaadi* cloth instead.

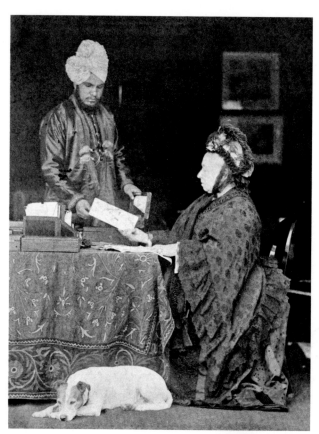

An 1897 photo of Abdul Karim and Queen Victoria. Karim earned the title of Munshi ("teacher") from the monarch.

Gandhi spent many years in prison for his agitation against the British, and he was a symbol for Hindu-Muslim unity in India. He also stood for the empowerment of lower-caste and untouchable Hindus. Gandhi's ideas of non-violent resistance inspired many people all over the world, including Nelson Mandela of South Africa and Martin Luther King, Jr., in America. In India, he is still called *bapu* ("father") and Mahatma ("great soul") out of respect.

Drained of its resources after World War II, Great Britain agreed to withdraw from South Asia in 1947.[5] India gained independence at midnight on August 15, a full twenty-four hours after East Pakistan and West Pakistan were created in the regions we know as Bangladesh and Pakistan today.

Mohandas Gandhi leads the way to the village of Dandi in 1930 to protest the salt production monopoly of the British. Gandhi believed in swaraj, or self-rule. He organized many movements against the British so India could be governed by Indians. His inspiration came from his Hindu religious beliefs.

Sunrise on the Ganga at Varanasi, one of the holy cities located along the river. The Ganga is mentioned in the most ancient of Hindu texts and is often worshipped as a goddess.

In the Shadow of the Himalayas

The mountains change colors when you see them from Tiger Hill.[1] Every morning the rays of the rising sun hit the Himalayas along a 150-mile-long (250 km) horizon, a sight that visitors make sure to witness from this viewpoint in the eastern Indian state of West Bengal. The early morning light makes the snow-capped peak of Mount Everest in the far distance on the Nepal-Tibet border appear sometimes pink, sometimes orange. The peaks of India's tallest mountain, Kanchenjunga, can also be seen from Tiger Hill, which rises to a spectacular 8,500 feet (2,590 meters) above sea level. This viewpoint is a UNESCO World Heritage Site and is located above Ghum, the highest railway station in India. The famous tea plantations of Darjeeling are only a few kilometers away.

Thirty of the world's highest peaks belong to the Himalayas.[2] Millions of years ago, when the earth and its continents looked quite different, the piece of land that would eventually form India's distinctive peninsular shape began to drift toward what is now Tibet. When the two land masses collided 30 million years ago, their edges pushed against each other, rose ever-higher, and became the Himalayas. This process continues today, and the Himalayas increase in height by a few millimeters each year.

The Himalayas swoop west to east for 1,553 miles (2,500 km) and separate South Asia from Central Asia. They also form India's northern border. Terrain often helps shape the identity and history of a people, and the Himalayas have been no different. Throughout history, these

At 28,169 feet (8,585 meters), Kanchenjunga is the highest mountain in India and the third highest peak in the world. It is located in the eastern Indian state of Sikkim and has held special religious significance for its people for centuries.

mountains have helped the people of South Asia maintain a distinct identity and protected themselves from outsiders. The Himalayas even feature heavily in the mythology of Indian religions, particularly Hinduism, Jainism, and Buddhism.

A horizontal stretch of fertile plains runs along the lower edge of the Himalayas. These are the Gangetic Plains, and they are the most densely populated parts of the country. The plains are named after the Ganga, the longest river in India. It originates in the Gangotri Glacier in the Himalayas and flows through the plains, depositing rich silt along its banks and making this region the most fertile in the country. The Brahmaputra and the Indus are two of India's other major river systems.

The landscape changes once again in the west where the land becomes arid. Western India is home to the Thar Desert of Rajasthan, south of which lie the marshes and salt flats of the Rann of Kutch in Gujarat. Pushkar in Rajasthan is the scene of a colorful camel fair

FYI FACT:

The Jim Corbett National Park near Nainital in north India is named after the British hunter who made his reputation by killing man-eating tigers in the early decades of the 20th century. He later became noted as a conservationist, naturalist, and writer. *The Man-Eaters of Kumaon* is one of his most famous books.

every year, and its cities are famous for their majestic Rajput forts and palaces. Hawa Mahal ("Palace of the Winds") in Jaipur dates back to 1798 and is one of the most famous sites in the area.

East of this region lies the Vindhya mountain range. For centuries, the Vindhyas have separated north India from the south.[3] Even today, these two regions are very different in their history, culture, and way of life. The Deccan Plateau lies south of the Vindhyas and forms most of the southern part of the Indian peninsula. In sharp contrast to the fertile soil of the Gangetic Plains in the north, the plateau is rocky and covered with black volcanic soil and crystalline rocks.

The green hills of the Western Ghats and the Eastern Ghats outline the plateau down to Kanniyakumari, the southernmost tip of the peninsula. At that point, visitors can see three great water bodies—the Indian Ocean, the Arabian Sea, and the Bay of Bengal—coming

Ghats in south India from the Kolli Hills in the state of Tamil Nadu

A Goan beach. Goa is located in the Western Ghats and was controlled by Portugal until 1961.

together in their various shades of blue.[4] Kanniyakumari is also well-known for the Gandhi Memorial, which is built so that the sun's rays fall upon the spot where his ashes used to be kept every year on his birthday.

India's 4,670-mile-long (7,516 km) coastline is a beach lover's dream. The sandy beaches of Goa and the idyllic backwaters of Kerala on the western coast are the most popular with tourists. The eastern coast is home to dense mangrove forests in West Bengal and Orissa. The Andamans and the Lakshadweep islands are famous for their beautiful coral reefs and attract those with a passion for water sports like snorkeling and scuba diving.

The climate in India varies with the terrain and the region, from temperate in the north to tropical in the south, but the country can be broadly thought of to experience three seasons: winter (October-March), summer (April-June), and several months of heavy rain and strong winds called the monsoon (July-September). Cherrapunji in the eastern state of Meghalaya holds the world record for the heaviest annual rainfall. Extreme weather often causes great destruction—the monsoon rains can bring floods and diseases like malaria and dengue. Cyclones devastate the eastern coast every year.

High-altitude hill towns like Munnar, Dalhousie, and Shimla were favorites of the Europeans during colonial times as a way of escaping the summer heat. Shimla was the summer capital of the British Raj.

The best place to experience India's rich wildlife is at sanctuaries, like the ones at Periyar in the south Indian state of Kerala and the Sunderbans in West Bengal. Environmentalists count 397 species of mammals, 1,250 species of birds, 460 species of reptiles, 240 species of amphibians, and 2,546 species of fish in India.[5] The most common animals are deer, antelope, goats, sheep, and primates like gibbons and langurs. Birds like barbets, sunbirds, parakeets, and magpies can be found almost everywhere. India recognizes the tiger as its national animal, but that hasn't prevented the animals from becoming an endangered species. Rhinoceroses and elephants also unfortunately join that list.

A wild Indian rhinoceros at the Kaziranga National Park. The park is located in the eastern Indian state of Assam.

The Rashtrapati Bhavan in New Delhi. The building was known as the Viceroy's House until 1950, when it was renamed. Rashtrapati Bhavan means "President's House."

Running a Democracy

While the sprawling pinkish-brown buildings at Delhi's Raisina Hill house India's political leaders today, they were built by the British when they ruled the country. Edwin Lutyens and Herbert Baker began to jointly design the buildings in and around Raisina Hill when the British Raj shifted its capital from Kolkata to Delhi in 1911.[1] It took 20 years to build New Delhi, the spacious new capital, which the British occupied for only 16 years. Today the president of India occupies the Rashtrapati Bhavan, an imposing domed structure that used to be the residence of the British viceroy of India. It is flanked on either side by the south and north blocks of the Secretariat, where the prime minister and important ministries have offices. The Indian constitution was drafted at the Sansad Bhavan, or Parliament House, located next door.

According to the constitution, India is a democratic republic. With a population of over a billion, India is the world's largest democracy. One out of every six people in the world is Indian. The Indian government marks the adoption of the constitution on January 26 when India became a republic in 1950, a day now celebrated as Republic Day. August 15 is celebrated as Independence Day. These two holidays, along with Gandhi Jayanti on October 2 (the birthday of the Mahatma) make up India's three national holidays.

Indian governance is patterned on the British parliamentary system and may be familiar to Americans as well.[3] However, unlike Britain and America where voters choose between two political parties, the

Barack Obama, the president of the United States, at the Sansad Bhavan in New Delhi in 2010. He is addressing a joint session of both houses of the Parliament of India.

citizens of India have many parties at their disposal. In a nation of diverse cultural identities, this usually leads to elections where no one party emerges as the political majority and coalition governments have to be formed.

The oldest and largest political party in India is the Indian National Congress (INC). It was founded in 1885 and played a major role during the struggle for independence.[2] It counted many of India's iconic founding fathers—Jawaharlal Nehru, Mahatma Gandhi, Abul Kalam Azad, and Vallabhbhai Patel—among its members. Another member, Dr. Bhimrao Ramji Ambedkar, drafted the Indian constitution.

The Bharatiya Janata Party (BJP, or the Indian People's Party) is the second-largest party. It was founded in 1980 and is known for its promotion of Hindu nationalism. The INC and the BJP are two of a handful of national parties with major representation across the country. They bolster their presence in parliament by forming alliances with any of a number of regional parties, like the All India Anna Dravida Munnetra Kazhagam (AIADMK) from the southern state of Tamil Nadu and the Samajwadi Party (SP) from the state of Uttar Pradesh in the north.[3]

The government is made up of the executive, legislative, and judicial branches. As the head of state, the president of India—who is chosen indirectly for a five-year term—heads the executive branch. The president works with the vice president and a cabinet called the Council of Ministers. The Council is headed by the prime minister, who is also the head of government.

The prime minister and the Council of Ministers are part of the legislative branch, which is divided into the upper house of the Rajya Sabha (Council of States) and the lower house of the Lok Sabha (House of the People). The 245 members of the Rajya Sabha are elected indirectly for six-year terms; each state is represented in proportion to its population. The Lok Sabha is made up of 545 members, of whom 543 are elected directly from India's constituencies for five-year terms. The remaining two members are appointed by the president from the Anglo-Indian community in case their representation falls short.

The president and the two houses together make up the Parliament of India. The prime minister is nominated by the president from the political party that has the most representation in the Lok Sabha. The term of the prime minister lasts for five years. The independent judiciary is made up of three levels: Supreme Court, 21 high courts, and many trial courts.

FYI FACT:

India's national anthem, "Jana Gana Mana," was composed by Rabindranath Tagore. Tagore is a famous Indian poet who in 1913 became the first non-European to win a Nobel Prize.

One presidential responsibility is overseeing the All India Civil Services. The organization's most famous face is that of Kiran Bedi. A native of Amritsar, Punjab, Bedi became the first female officer to be inducted into the Indian Police Service (IPS) in 1972. Some people remember her as "Crane Bedi," who had the car of then-prime minister Indira Gandhi towed for a traffic violation in 1982! In 1994, she won a Ramon Magsaysay Award for her prison reforms in Delhi's Tihar jail. She retired from the IPS in 2007, but she remained active as a leading figure in India's fight against corruption.

The Nehru-Gandhis (no relation to the Mahatma) are India's premier political dynasty. Jawaharlal Nehru's daughter Indira Gandhi and grandson Rajiv Gandhi also served as prime minister. Today, Rajiv Gandhi's Italian-born widow Sonia heads the Congress Party. Many believe that her son Rahul will become prime minister some day.

Indira Gandhi

The president is in charge of the Indian military, which includes the army, navy, and air force. In addition, the president oversees the Indian Coast Guard, the Special Frontier Force, the Assam Rifles, and the Strategic Forces Command. India has the third-largest military in the world, ranking behind China and the United States. It spends a considerable amount of its defenses on its borders with Pakistan, with whom it went to war in 1947, 1965, 1971, and 1999. India also fought a war with China in 1962.

India's foreign relations are in accordance with the Non-Aligned Movement, whose members do not align themselves with or against any major power bloc in the world.[4] Still, India faces disputes over the land and its resources, especially along its borders with some of its neighbors such as China, Pakistan, Bangladesh, Nepal, and Sri Lanka. Violence and bloodshed mark these disputed areas. Tourists generally avoid these regions, which can be dangerous to visitors and locals both.

Workers in an electronics company perform quality control on an assembly line. India is one of the largest and fastest growing economies in the world. It faces no shortage of labor and much of its population speaks English.

The Business of Money

Nobody would have heard of the seaside village of Dandi had it not been for Mahatma Gandhi. On April 6, 1930, he brought his *satyagraha* ("struggle for the truth") against the British Raj to this sleepy town along the Arabian Sea after walking 240 miles (390 km) in 24 days. Seventy-eight of his followers had walked with him all the way. At the edge of what is now the state of Gujarat, Gandhi defied the British Raj by picking up a handful of salt from the beach.[1] In those days, only the British were allowed to make salt in India. Salt was a precious resource, and whoever controlled its production had the Indian economy in their hands.

The Indian economy has come a long way since then, but some things remain the same. Gandhi once said that India's soul was in its villages. With over half the Indian labor force working in agriculture, he may have been right, but for reasons best left to economists, agriculture forms just a small part of India's Gross Domestic Product (GDP). Sixty-five percent of India's GDP comes from the services sector, 18 percent from industry, and only 17 percent from agriculture. India has the second-largest labor force in the world, more than three times the size of the United States.[2] Mumbai is considered the financial capital. The city contributes a significant portion of India's GDP and is where financial institutions like the Reserve Bank of India and the National Stock Exchange are located. Dalal ("Broker") Street in Mumbai is the equivalent of Wall Street in New York City.

Jawaharlal Nehru chose to take India down a path different from Gandhi's vision of a village-based economy. In the crucial early years of independence, Nehru laid down an industry-based model of development containing both socialist and capitalist features. Development goals were set in a series of five-year-plans, a practice that continues to this day. Nehru wanted India to be self-sufficient in all of its needs. Perhaps this attitude was born out of the memory of India's earlier subjugation to the British. Today, the Indian economy heavily depends on industries such as textiles, chemicals, food processing, construction, transportation, software, and pharmaceuticals. The country has 352 airports and the fourth largest railway network in the world (a legacy of the British Raj).[3]

The Indian economy has opened up considerably to foreign businesses since the 1990s when India made changes to its economic policies. The architect of the new economy was then-Finance Minister

Workers assemble a Maxximo mini-truck at the newly inaugurated Mahindra and Mahindra India plant at Chakan, some 100 miles (160 kilometers) southeast of Mumbai. The company is one of India's largest vehicle manufacturers.

Dr. Manmohan Singh (who became prime minister in 2004). The Indian economy is more capitalist now. A number of industries have been privatized, and government regulation on both local and foreign businesses has reduced. This has made India one of the fastest-growing economies in the world. In 2010, it stayed safe from the global financial crisis due to its conservative business practices.

The telecommunications industry in particular has undergone explosive growth.[4] India has the third-largest internet user population and the second-largest cell-phone user population in the world, greater

Employees of a call center in India deal with international customers on the telephone.

than the United States. There are over 700 satellite television channels in India. That's a far cry from the government-run Doordarshan, which was India's only television channel until the early 1990s.

Today, India is the preferred outsourcing hub of most Western countries. The biggest reason for this is that Indian workers cost less money and also speak English. Thanks to its colonial past, India is the largest English-speaking country in the world. This gives Indian workers an edge over other upcoming economic giants like China and Brazil.

Some of the top employers in India today are foreign multi-national corporations. Companies like Google and Microsoft have a strong presence on university campuses and are known to aggressively hire new graduates. Some traditional employers remain popular in India as well. Indian Railways and the armed forces are the top employers in

In recognition of Indian's worldwide economic importance, the Indian rupee received its own international symbol (₹) in 2010. It joins other well-known symbols such as the dollar ($), pound (£), and euro (€). Rupee comes from a Sanskrit word that means silver.

India. While the unemployment rate was less than three percent in 2013, it had risen slightly in the past few years.[5]

The United Arab Emirates, United States, and China are India's top trading partners. India exports petroleum products, precious stones, machinery, iron and steel, chemicals, vehicles, and apparel. Its main imports include crude oil, precious stones, machinery, fertilizer, iron and steel, and chemicals. India is the fourth-largest provider of coal in the world. It also has abundant sources of minerals, natural gas, diamonds, petroleum, and limestone.

Nariman Point, in Mumbai's central business district, has some of the world's most expensive office spaces.

Unfortunately, about 65 percent of India's land has been degraded by pollution, overuse, and mismanagement.[6] No city in India receives a continuous water supply and less than 10 percent of cities have a sewage system. Over 75 percent of the country's surface water is contaminated. Power outages occur, an inconvenience in a country with extreme climatic conditions.

Red tape and bureaucratic delays are still a part of the economy, and dealing with a corrupt system is part of life for all Indians and even visitors. Indian law officials are said to be among the most corrupt in the world.[7] Many accuse the police of replacing India's old British masters. Impoverished individuals from India's farming communities frequently get exploited and end up resorting to suicide in desperation, a problem that has persisted since the days of Gandhi.

FYI FACT:

India's White Revolution was the world's biggest dairy development program. It made India the largest dairy producer in the world and pulled the country out of dairy deficiency in 1998.

A vendor sells vegetables at the Sarojini Nagar market in New Delhi. Indians traditionally buy their groceries from vendors such as these, who gather at farmers' markets called mandis. Other vendors carry their fruits, vegetables, and snacks on moving carts and sell them by the road or between neighborhoods.

An Indian Life

Nowhere is India's disparity between the rich and poor more glaring than in Mumbai, the financial and entertainment capital of the country. Dharavi, one of the largest slums in the world, lies only a few kilometers away from the Chhatrapati Shivaji International Airport. Over a million people are thought to live in Dharavi. Some were hired as actors for the 2008 Oscar Best Picture winner, *Slumdog Millionaire*. Parts of the movie were filmed in the slum.

Most foreigners feel unsettled and even upset by the extreme poverty in which a large chunk of India's population lives. As of 2010, almost one-third of the population lived below the poverty line (under $1.25 a day).[1] Over half were below two dollars a day. And the number keeps growing—India adds the equivalent of the population of Australia (more than 22 million) every year! India is the second-most populated country in the world.

Life, however, goes on for the country's 1.2 billion people, and surprisingly with more gusto than almost anywhere else in the world. In 2012, according to an international survey, "Indonesia scores the happiest out of the 24 countries surveyed with just over half (51%) of citizens reporting they are 'very happy' followed by India and Mexico at 43% each."[2] By contrast, the United States ranked 8th at 28%. This lofty ranking may be because Indian culture places great emphasis on relationships and community. Many children grow up in joint families, where an entire extended family—including grandparents, uncles, aunts, and cousins—lives under one roof. Even when children live with their

How many of these famous people of Indian origin do you know? Astronaut Kalpana Chawla, filmmakers M. Knight Shyamalan and Satyajit Ray, author Salman Rushdie, politician Bobby Jindal, actress Parminder Nagra, actor Ben Kingsley, comedian Russell Peters, and rock star Freddie Mercury.

parents in nuclear families (like in the United States), they prefer to have their relatives nearby.

Social interaction between men and women is generally not encouraged in India. In many rural areas, the women wear veils to hide their faces from men. People in the cities wear Western clothes more often, but a large part of India still prefers traditional and more conservative clothing. Fashion varies greatly across the Indian landscape, but *saris* and *shalwar* suits are the most popular with women. Men wear loose *kurta* pajamas or *dhoti kurtas*. Tourists can pick up an entire wardrobe (but with a good round of haggling) at street shops in every city. The Delhi bazaars of Sarojini Nagar and Lajpat Nagar are an experience in themselves. For the less adventurous are the many American-style malls that have sprung up in India's larger cities. The government-run state emporiums in Delhi are the best place to sample handicrafts from every state.

India's innumerable dining options and unfamiliar flavors may overwhelm the new tourist. Food preparations vary by region (and sometimes by neighborhood) according to terrain and religion. Most dishes are served with different kinds of *roti* (flatbread) or rice. Indian restaurants in the United States carry many of India's

A typical multi-generational Indian family wearing traditional clothes.

signature dishes, like *daals* (lentils), kebabs, biryanis, and endless combinations of vegetables and meat cooked with spices from various parts of the country. Desserts like *gulaab jaamun*, *payasum*, *jalebi*, and *sandesh* include sugar, milk, and *ghee* (a form of butter) among other ingredients and are very rich. Indian people prefer to eat with their right hand, although it may take foreigners a few tries to copy the way they eat with their fingers.

Food forms a large part of important ceremonies in India such as weddings. Marriages in India are arranged by the extended family. Appropriate matches are found from similar religious and regional backgrounds, although cross-cultural "love" marriages and even live-in relationships are not unusual in the larger cities. Friendships are close, particularly with those of one's own gender. Many foreigners find it confusing when they see two Indian men holding hands in public!

Children can go to any number of government, international, and religious schools. Parents can even choose to home-school their children. The Indian education system, with its stress on mathematics and the sciences, is extremely competitive and churns out a large number of doctors and engineers. Working life can be exhausting. Most Indians—both men and an increasing number of women—work long hours and sometimes seven days a week to make ends meet.

As a result, they especially appreciate India's stress-busters—movies and sports. Films provide an escape from the worries of daily life. India's rich linguistic heritage has spawned a dazzling entertainment industry. Hindi is the most widely understood language, but the constitution recognizes 14 other languages amongst the hundreds that are spoken across the country.[3] Ironically, English, the language of the British, helps to unify this country of many languages. Many Indians understand at least English, Hindi, and their mother tongue.

In India, cricket leaves the arts behind. Important matches can feel like national events. In 2011, when India won the ICC Cricket World Cup for the first time since 1983, people all across the country erupted onto the streets and celebrated all night. India may not have a national sport, but cricket is certainly the most popular game in the country. It often feels like the only sport in India!

Overcrowding and poor sanitation in India give rise to diseases like diarrhea, hepatitis, typhoid, dengue, and malaria. Many visitors often develop stomach problems, a phenomenon called "Delhi Belly."

Mumbai native Sachin Tendulkar is widely known in the international cricket world. His status among his fans, who affectionately call him "Little Master" because of his youthful appearance, is almost godly. "Cricket is my religion, Sachin is my god," they like to say. Tendulkar is also known as "Master Blaster" because of his skills as a record-shattering batsman. Tourists quickly learn to recognize him

India's Hindi-language film industry in Mumbai, more commonly known as Bollywood (after the city's old name, Bombay), produces the highest number of movies in the world. Some of its most well-known actors are Shahrukh Khan, Aishwarya Rai, Aamir Khan, Amitabh Bachchan, and Irfan Khan. Ravi Shankar (father of the singer Norah Jones), Zubin Mehta, and A.R. Rehman are world-famous for their musical talents. The late M.F. Husain is India's most recognizable artist.

India's Ravindra Jadeja bats as Zimbabwe captain Brendan Taylor watches the wicket during a cricket match at the Queens Sports Club in Harare, Zimbabwe, on August 3, 2013.

from his image on billboards, television commercials, and print ads. India has formally honored him with a number of awards, like the Padma Vibhushan in 2008, which is the second highest civilian award in the country. He is also an honorary member of the Order of Australia.

Field hockey, badminton, tennis, and soccer are also popular in India. Leander Paes and Mahesh Bhupathi formed an award-winning international doubles tennis team for many years, and Sania Mirza also made a name for herself in the sport. Many Indian children look up to India's sportspeople, like badminton star Saina Nehwal, golfer Jeev Milkha Singh, boxer Vijender Kumar, chess master Vishwanathan Anand, and soccer idol Baichung Bhutia. Sprinter Milkha Singh, who competed in three Olympics, ran so fast that he is still called The Flying Sikh!

At the end of the day, life in an overcrowded country can be challenging. In addition to the problems of crime, disease, and pollution, Indian society suffers from a host of problems. Discrimination on the basis of gender, language, religion, region, and even skin color is serious enough for many regions to demand statehood and even independence from India. Many families prefer sons over daughters, and this has dangerously skewed the national sex ratio. Women have a difficult time asserting their rights because of problems like female infanticide, dowry-related bridal murders, sexual harassment (known in India as "eve-teasing"), and honor killings. Tourists, particularly females, are often advised to travel in groups in well-lit areas. Like everything else, diversity and an ancient heritage come with a dark side.

One of the 14 gopurams, or gateway towers, of the Sri Meenakshi Temple in Madurai, Tamil Nadu. Gopurams are signature features of Hindu temples in southern India. The Sri Meenakshi temple is dedicated to an incarnation of the Hindu goddess Parvati and her consort, the god Shiva.

All Roads
Lead to God

Space and silence can be hard to come by in any of India's metropolises...except perhaps at the Baha'i House of Worship in New Delhi. More commonly referred to as the Lotus Temple, this UNESCO World Heritage Site was designed to look like a lotus flower. Nine pools surround the white marble temple, quietly reflecting back the serenity of its 27 petals to itself and to the world. Beautifully trimmed gardens cover 227 acres (92 hectares). Services, which are open to all, include Persian Baha'i hymns and verses from other faiths.

The American writer Mark Twain once remarked that "in religion, all other countries are paupers. India is the only millionaire."[1] Over 80 percent of Indians are Hindus, and the next largest religious group in India consists of Muslims. Indians can also be Christian, Jewish, Zoroastrian, Sikh, Jain, or Buddhist. Many Indians also believe in astrology, numerology, and black magic. The government itself is secular, but because life without religion is almost unthinkable to most Indians, special laws have been created for some religious groups to deal with issues like marriage, divorce, and inheritance.[2]

Hinduism has much in common with the traditions of the ancient Greeks, Romans, and Egyptians.[3] Many historians believe that "Hinduism" comes from the word ancient foreigners used to refer to the various beliefs of the people scattered across South Asia. Hindus believe in the existence of (some say) millions of gods, goddesses, and other divine beings. No one person founded the religion, and its philosophies are contained within a series of scriptures composed over the ages. The most important scriptures are the Vedas, the Upanishads, the Puranas, and the great epics—the Mahabharata and the Ramayana. Part of the Mahabharata is called the Bhagavad Gita and contains psalm-like wisdom from the god Krishna. Time is thought to run in a circle in a series of ages. Instead of prophets, the gods themselves appear in human form as avatars to help the people on earth.

The terrain of India seems to have found its way as symbols in Hinduism. A number of stories in Hindu mythology take place in the Himalayas, and a divine mountain called Meru is believed to be the center of the Hindu universe. A number of important Hindu temples, Buddhist monasteries, and other spiritual retreats are located in the Himalayas. The best-known is the town of Rishikesh in the northern state of Uttarakhand. It became famous in the 1960s when the Beatles visited it. Today, it is known as the Yoga Capital of the World.[4]

The Ganga river, which originates in the Himalayas, is also considered sacred by the Hindus. Varanasi (also called Kashi) in Uttar Pradesh, a city on the banks of the river, is an important Hindu pilgrimage site.[5] Worshippers visit Varanasi to bathe their sins away in the holy water of the Ganga. The Hindus cremate their dead; many desire to have their ashes scattered into the Ganga. They also believe in reincarnation and that good deeds promise a better next life until the soul attains freedom from the cycle of rebirth.

The Baha'i House of Worship in New Delhi was built in 1986 in the shape of a lotus flower. The Baha'i religion was founded in Persia in the 19th century.

A view of Rishikesh across the Laxman Jhula bridge.

Hindu society is divided into four *varnas* or castes: Brahmins (priests), Kshatriyas (warriors and rulers), Vaishyas (scribes and merchants), and Shudras (laborers). At the bottom of Hindu society are the Dalits (untouchables). These castes are further broken down into *jatis*.[6] Castes were originally based on occupation but have now become very rigid; people cannot change their *varna* or *jati*. Hinduism also does not accept converts or those who have renounced the faith and seek to return. While caste-based discrimination and exploitation is now against the law, the problem still persists. Inter-caste marriages are frowned upon. In extreme cases, people have been killed for marrying into the wrong caste. The strict social hierarchy has also influenced other religious communities.

A large part of India's culture is influenced by its religious makeup. Hinduism considers dance, singing, and music a form of worship and is responsible for India's rich heritage in the performing arts. Some of India's most recognizable dance forms—like Kathak, Bharatnatyam, Odissi, and Manipuri—enact stories from Hindu mythology.[7]

Classical Indian music can be broadly classified as Hindustani (north Indian) and Carnatic (south Indian). Hindustani music was

FYI FACT:

The swastika used by German dictator Adolf Hitler as a symbol of his Nazi Party before and during World War II was borrowed from Hinduism. The original symbol is considered sacred and meant to bring good luck.

inspired by ancient Hindu Vedic chants and the music of the Persians. Muslim Sufi music is also popular and sung with great passion at *dargahs* across India. *Dargahs* are shrines built over the graves of Sufi saints and visited by both Hindus and Muslims.

Indian cuisine varies with religion. Not all Hindus are vegetarians, but none eat beef because they consider the cow as a sacred animal. Muslims don't eat pork but Christians do. Jains avoid vegetables like onions, potatoes, and garlic that grow under the ground. Some vegetarians don't even eat eggs.

India's religious splendor is best witnessed in its architecture. The sprawling Sri Meenakshi temple complex in Madurai, Tamil Nadu, is famous for its ornate gateways, the tallest of which stretches upward to 170 feet (52 meters).[8] The gods have been captured in stone at ancient Buddhist cave sculptures at Ajanta and Buddhist, Jain, and Hindu rock sculptures at Ellora, both of which are in the western state of Maharashtra and are UNESCO

The Ajanta caves in Aurangabad, Maharashtra. Three hundred Buddhist monuments were cut into these caves between the 2nd century BCE and the 6th century CE.

The Harmandir Sahib (also known as the Golden Temple) in Amritsar, Punjab.

World Heritage Sites.[9] Another World Heritage Site is the Mahabodhi Temple at Bodh Gaya, Bihar, where the Buddha is believed to have attained enlightenment.

Arches, domes, and calligraphy—the art of fine or ornate handwriting—were introduced to India by the Muslims. These are a common feature of Muslim places of worship, the largest one in India being the Jama Masjid in New Delhi. The Golden Temple in Amritsar, Punjab, is a Sikh *gurudwara* and combines both Hindu and Muslim styles. India's Christian heritage can be seen in the beautiful Portuguese churches in Goa and French churches in Puducherry. A synagogue forms the center of Jew Town in Cochin, Kerala, where a small Jewish community still thrives. Many fire temples, where India's Zoroastrian community worships, are located in Mumbai.

India may only observe three secular national holidays, but state governments can choose to observe a number of religious festivals. Many Hindu festivals like Pongal and Lohri are agricultural in nature, while Diwali, Holi, and Dussehra honor the gods. Raksha Bandhan celebrates the brother-sister relationship. Other major Indian festivals are Islamic (Ramadan, Eid al Fitr, and Eid al Adha) and Christian (Christmas and Easter). That's a lot of holidays for schoolchildren!

India's religious diversity has a downside. Superstition is common, and tensions among various religious communities can get ugly. Christian missionaries are looked upon with suspicion by conservative Hindus, and many places have been scarred by Hindu-Muslim clashes. In recent times, Gujarat, the birthplace of Gandhi—the champion of communal harmony—has been the scene of horrendous violence between the Hindus and the Muslims.

Tandoori Chicken

The Mughals take the credit for bringing tandoori chicken to the Indian palate. Tandoors are cylindrical clay ovens in which food is cooked by exposing it to direct heat from a coal or wood fire that has been lit on the inside. These ovens are kept lit for hours at a time; their inner temperature can be as high as 900°F (480°C). Let your standard kitchen stove stand in for the fiery tandoor for this delicious Mughal tradition.

Ingredients:

- 1 pound chicken legs
- 3 tablespoons lemon juice
- 2 teaspoons salt
- 1 teaspoon paprika
- ¼ teaspoon red chili powder
- 1½ teaspoons coriander powder
- 1 teaspoon cumin
- ½ teaspoon yellow or red food coloring
- ½ cup yogurt
- 1 teaspoon garlic paste
- 1 teaspoon minced ginger
- Cooking oil spray
- Sliced lemons, cucumbers, onions

Instructions:

1. Wash the chicken legs, and cut slits into them with a knife.
2. In a bowl, mix the lemon juice, salt, paprika, red chili powder, coriander powder, cumin, and food coloring into a dry paste.
3. Rub the mixture onto the chicken with your hands and let it sit for 15 minutes in a wide dish.
4. In a bowl, mix the yogurt, garlic paste, and ginger.
5. Pour the mixture onto the chicken, making sure it is well-coated. Let the chicken sit in the marinade overnight, or at least for 5 hours.
6. Pre-heat the oven to 350°F.
7. Cover a baking tray with aluminum foil and spray the foil with a light layer of oil.
8. Place the chicken on the aluminum foil and spray it with a light layer of oil.
9. Bake the chicken for 30–40 minutes until well-cooked. Carefully turn it over once or twice to make sure it bakes evenly.
10. Serve hot with sliced lemons, cucumbers, and onions.

Henna

Tattoo

Henna tattoos aren't really tattoos. They are temporary designs that can be made on the skin with dye made from plants. Many people also use henna to color their hair. Traditionally used by women in Asia, Africa, and the Middle East as a cosmetic during weddings and festivals, henna art has grown popular with both men and women in the Western world. This is one tattoo your parents won't have a problem with!

Materials
- Henna powder
- Water
- Bowl
- Stiff paintbrush
- Lemon juice
- Cotton balls

Instructions
1. In the bowl, mix the henna powder with enough water to make a smooth paste.
2. Dip the paintbrush in the henna paste and carefully draw a design on your skin. Complete the design.
3. Let the paste dry on your skin for a few hours. Use a cotton ball to lightly dab some lemon juice on the design. This will prevent the paste from drying too fast and help dye your skin better.
4. When the paste has dried, rub it off your skin. Don't use soap on that part of your body for 24 hours.

TIMELINE

Dates BCE

c. 2500–1500 The Indus Valley civilization flourishes in northwestern India.

c. 2000–500 India's Vedic Period; the Hindu Vedas are compiled.

322–182 The Mauryan Empire rises and thrives; its greatest ruler, Ashoka, reigns from 272 to 232.

Dates CE

320 The Gupta Period ushers in the Golden Age of India; it ends about 550.

1206 The Delhi Sultanate establishes Muslim control over part of India; it lasts until 1526.

1336 The Hindu Vijayanagar Empire begins and dominates central and south India for more than 200 years.

1526 The Mughal Empire controls much of India before coming to an end in 1857.

1600 Queen Elizabeth I grants a trade charter to the East India Company.

1632 Shah Jahan begins construction of the Taj Mahal as a memorial to his deceased wife.

1857 British troops crush the Great Indian Mutiny.

1914–1918 Indian soldiers fight in every major theatre of operations during World War I.

1920 Mahatma Gandhi begins his civil disobedience campaign.

1939–1945 Indian troops fight for Britain during World War II.

1947 India becomes independent on August 15 and soon afterward is involved in a war with Pakistan that lasts until the following December.

1948 Mahatma Gandhi is assassinated; India and Pakistan battle over Kashmir.

1950 India becomes a republic on January 26.

1962 Border tensions with China lead to the Sino-Indian War.

1965 India fights a second war with Pakistan, primarily over Kashmir.

1971 India's third war with Pakistan is over East Pakistan (now Bangladesh).

1974 India tests its first nuclear device in Pokhran, Rajasthan.

1975 Prime Minister Indira Gandhi declares a state of emergency that lasts for two years.

1984 Indira Gandhi is assassinated by Sikh separatists; her son, Rajiv Gandhi, becomes prime minister and Hindu-Sikh riots ensue.

1991 Rajiv Gandhi is assassinated.

1992 A Hindu mob tears down a Muslim mosque in Ayodhya, Uttar Pradesh; Hindu-Muslim violence spreads across the country.

1999 The fourth India-Pakistan war centers on Kargil, Kashmir.

2000 India marks the birth of its billionth citizen.

2002 Hindu-Muslim clashes in the state of Gujarat kill thousands.

2008	India launches its first lunar mission; Pakistani gunmen attack several targets in Mumbai, killing at least 100 people.
2010	India hosts the 19th Commonwealth Games in Delhi and finishes third in total medal count behind Australia and England.
2011	Social activist Anna Hazare stages a hunger strike in Delhi to protest corruption, and the government quickly accepts his demands.
2013	India passes Japan to become the world's third-largest internet population.
2014	India's jewellery imports rise due to a shortage of gold.

CHAPTER NOTES

Chapter 1. Overview of India

1. "Great Speeches of the 20th Century," *The Guardian*, April 30, 2007. http://www.guardian.co.uk/theguardian/2007/may/01/greatspeeches
2. Pippa de Bruyn et. al., *Frommer's India* (Hoboken, New Jersey: Wiley Publishing, 2010), p. 28.

Chapter 2. Ancient Invasions

1. Abigail Hole et. al., *Discover India* (Oakland, Cal.: Lonely Planet Publications, 2011), pp. 97–98.
2. "Winston Churchill." Encyclopaedia Britannica. http://www.britannica.com/EBchecked/topic/117269/Sir-Winston-Churchill/117269suppinfo/Supplemental-Information
3. Hole et.al, *Discover India*, p. 395.
4. Ibid.
5. Ibid., pp. 396–397.
6. Ibid., pp. 97–98.

Chapter 3. Muslims, Europeans, and Nationhood

1. Roshen Dalal et al., *India* (New York: Dorling Kindersley, 2011), pp. 530–533.
2. Abigail Hole et al., *Discover India* (Oakland, Cal.: Lonely Planet Publications, 2011), p. 398.
3. Pippa de Bruyn et al., *Frommer's India* (Hoboken, New Jersey: Wiley Publishing, 2010), pp. 428–429.
4. Ibid., p. 26.
5. Dalal et. al., *India*, p. 56.

Chapter 4. In the Shadow of the Himalayas

1. Abigail Hole et. al., *Discover India* (Oakland, Cal.: Lonely Planet Publications, 2011), pp. 310–311.
2. Ibid., pp. 64–65.
3. Ibid., p. 548.
4. Ibid.
5. Ibid., pp. 422–424.

Chapter 5. Running a Democracy

1. Abigail Hole et. al., *Discover India* (Oakland, Cal.: Lonely Planet Publications, 2011), pp. 72–74.
2. Pippa de Bruyn et.al., *Frommer's India* (Hoboken, New Jersey: Wiley Publishing, 2010), p. 27.
3. CIA: *The World Factbook*, "India." https://www.cia.gov/library/publications/the-world-factbook/geos/in.html
4. Ibid.

Chapter 6. The Business of Money

1. Pippa de Bruyn et. al., *Frommer's India* (Hoboken, New Jersey: Wiley Publishing, 2010), p. 28.
2. CIA: *The World Factbook*: India. https://www.cia.gov/library/publications/the-world-factbook/geos/in.html
3. Ibid.
4. Ibid.
5. N.D. Shiva Kumar, "Unemployment rate rises in India," *Times of India*, June 23, 2013.http://articles.timesofindia.indiatimes.com/2013-06-23/india 40146190_1_urban-india-urban-women-rural-women
6. Abigail Hole et. al., *Discover India* (Oakland, Cal.: Lonely Planet Publications, 2011), p. 423.
7. de Bruyn et. al., *Frommer's India*, pp. 17–21.

Chapter 7. An Indian Life

1. CIA: *The World Factbook*, "India." https://www.cia.gov/library/publications/the-world-factbook/geos/in.html
2. "Despite Woes, Conflicts, World a Happier Place than in 2007 as 22% (+2 points) of Global Citizens Say They're 'Very Happy,'" IPSOS, February 9, 2012. http://www.ipsos-na.com/news-polls/pressrelease.aspx?id=5515
3. CIA: *The World Factbook*, "India." https://www.cia.gov/library/publications/the-world-factbook/geos/in.html

Chapter 8. All Roads Lead to God

1. "Mark Twain's Little Known Travels in India." *Hinduism Today*, April 1996. http://www.hinduismtoday.com/modules/smartsection/item.php?itemid=3610
2. CIA: *The World Factbook*, "India." https://www.cia.gov/library/publications/the-world-factbook/geos/in.html
3. John Bowker, *World Religions* (New York: Dorling Kindersley, 2003), pp. 20–43.
4. Abigail Hole et. al., *Discover India* (Oakland, Cal.: Lonely Planet Publications, 2011), p. 352.
5. Roshen Dalal et al., *India* (New York: Dorling Kindersley, 2011), pp. 202–209.
6. Hole et. al., *Discover India*, p. 409.
7. Dalal et. al., *India*, pp. 28–29.
8. Hole et. al., *Discover India*, p. 282.
9. Pippa de Bruyn et. al, *Frommer's India* (Hoboken, New Jersey: Wiley Publishing, 2010), pp. 182–190.

Books

365 Tales from Indian Mythology. Noida, India: Om Books International, 2006.

Dalal, Roshen. *The Puffin History of India for Children, Volume 1*. New Delhi, India: Penguin Books India, 2002.

Dalal, Roshen. *The Puffin History of India for Children, Volume 2*. New Delhi, India: Penguin Books India, 2003.

Ejaz, Khadija. *Meet Our New Student from India*. Hockessin, Del.: Mitchell Lane Publishers, 2009.

Ejaz, Khadija. *Recipe and Craft Guide to India*. Hockessin, Del.: Mitchell Lane Publishers, 2010.

Nehru, Jawaharlal. *Letters from a Father to His Daughter*. New York: Viking Press, 2004.

Srinivasan, Radhika, Leslie Jermyn, and Rosaline Lum. *India: Cultures of the World*. Tarrytown, New York: Marshall Cavendish Benchmark, 2012.

On the Internet

BBC News—India Country Profile
http://www.bbc.co.uk/news/world-south-asia-12557384

Incredible India!
http://www.incredibleindia.org/

Sanskrita Pradipika
http://www.sanskrit-lamp.org

WORKS CONSULTED

Asia Map, worldatlas.com, http://www.worldatlas.com/webimage/countrys/as.htm

Bowker, John. *World Religions*. New York, New York: Dorling Kindersley, 2003.

CIA: The World Factbook: India
https://www.cia.gov/library/publications/the-world-factbook/geos/in.html

Crossette, Barbara. *India: Facing the Twenty-First Century*. Bloomington, Indiana: Indiana University Press, 1993.

Dalal, Roshen et.al. *India*. New York: Dorling Kindersley, 2011.

Desai, Kalpana, and Joseph St. Anne. *The Museum Guidebook*. Mumbai, India: Chhatrapati Shivaji Maharaj Vastu Sangrahalaya, 2010.

de Bruyn, Pippa et. al. *Frommer's India*. Hoboken, New Jersey: Wiley Publishing, Inc., 2010.

Hole, Abigail et.al. *Discover India*. Oakland, California: Lonely Planet Publications, 2011.

"Mark Twain's Little Known Travels in India." *Hinduism Today*, April 1996.
http://www.hinduismtoday.com/modules/smartsection/item.php?itemid=3610

Shiva Kumar, N.D."Unemployment rate rises in India," *Times of India*, June 23, 2013.
http://articles.timesofindia.indiatimes.com/2013-06-23/india/40146190_1_
urban-india-urban-women-rural-women

agitation (aa-juh-TAY-shun)—The act of attempting to stir up public opinion.

Anglo-Indian (ANG-gloe IN-dee-uh)—A person of joint English and Indian descent.

arid (AYR-id)—Having little or no rain.

boycott (BOY-kaht)—To refuse to do business with a company or organization.

bureaucratic (BYO-ruh-kra-tik)—Rigidly devoted to the details of administrative procedure.

cabinet (KAB-i-net)—A group of ministers who make government policies.

capitalist (KAP-i-ta-list)—An economic system based on private ownership of the means of production.

coalition (ko-uh-LISH-un)—An alliance or union between groups.

corrode (koh-ROAD)—To deteriorate by chemical reaction.

cremation (kree-MAY-shun)—The act of burning a dead body to ashes.

dowry (DOW-ree)—Money or property brought by a bride to her husband at marriage.

enlightenment (en-LAI-ten-ment)—The awakening to ultimate truth.

epic (EH-pik)—A long poem centered upon a hero's achievements.

evangelism (ee-VAN-jehl-izm)—Spreading the word about a religion.

infanticide (in-FAN-tuh-side)—The practice of killing newborn infants.

mangrove (MAN-grove)—A tropical tree that grows in marshes or tidal shores.

minaret (min-uh-REHT)—A slender tower attached to a mosque.

mythology (mih-THAH-luh-jee)—A collection of myths belonging to a group, usually religious or cultural in nature.

nationalism (NAA-shuh-nahl-izm)—Devotion to one's country.

outsourcing (OUT-sore-sing)—Obtaining services or products from an outside supplier.

pilgrim (PIL-grihm)—A religious devotee who journeys to a shrine or sacred place.

plantation (plan-TAY-shun)—A large estate where crops are raised by resident workers.

reincarnation (ree-in-kar-NAY-shun)—Rebirth of the soul in another form of life.

socialist (SOH-sha-list)—An economic system based on government ownership of the means of production.

Sufi (SOO-fee)—Relating to Islamic mysticism.

sultan (SUHL-tun)—A ruler of a Muslim country.

INDEX

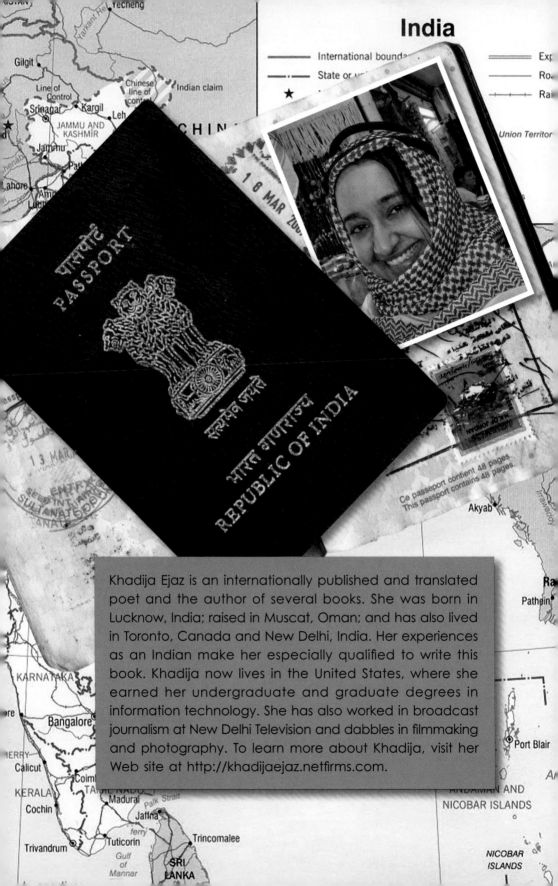

Khadija Ejaz is an internationally published and translated poet and the author of several books. She was born in Lucknow, India; raised in Muscat, Oman; and has also lived in Toronto, Canada and New Delhi, India. Her experiences as an Indian make her especially qualified to write this book. Khadija now lives in the United States, where she earned her undergraduate and graduate degrees in information technology. She has also worked in broadcast journalism at New Delhi Television and dabbles in filmmaking and photography. To learn more about Khadija, visit her Web site at http://khadijaejaz.netfirms.com.